Dolphin
Adventure

Paola
Marquez

Other Books by
Wayne Grover

DOLPHIN FREEDOM
DOLPHIN TREASURE

Paola
Marquez

Dolphin Adventure

a True Story

Wayne Grover

Illustrated by Jim Fowler

HarperTrophy®
A Division of HarperCollinsPublishers

Harper Trophy® is a registered trademark of HarperCollins Publishers Inc.

Dolphin Adventure
Text copyright © 1990 by Wayne Grover
Illustrations copyright © 1990 by Jim Fowler

For information address HarperCollins Children's Books, a division of
HarperCollins Publishers, 1350 Avenue of the Americas, New York, NY 10019.

Library of Congress Cataloging-in-Publication Data
Grover, Wayne.
 Dolphin adventure, a true story / by Wayne Grover.
 p. cm.
 Summary: A diver describes how he encounters and gains the trust of a family of
dolphins and saves the life of their baby.
 ISBN 0-380-73252-1 (pbk.)
 1. Dolphins—Juvenile literature. [1. Dolphins. 2. Wildlife rescue.] I. Fowler, Jim
ill. II. Title.
QL795D7G76 1990   89-27226
599.5'3—dc20   CIP
                                                                     AC

First Harper Trophy edition, 2000

Visit us on the World Wide Web!
www.harperchildrens.com

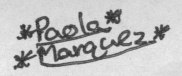

Paola
Marquez

This story is dedicated
to the children of the world,
so they may share the beauty of
the sea's underwater creatures

—W. G.

In memory of
my brother, Mike

—J. F.

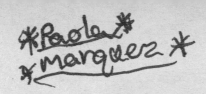

Contents

Dolphin
Adventure

Chapter One

A Special Day

The Florida sun warmed our backs as we loaded the diving gear aboard our boat. It was a cool winter morning in South Florida, the kind my friends and I liked best. Several pelicans sat on nearby dock pilings, watching, looking for a bite of food they might beg from us.

Because the air was cool and the sea was warm, a foggy mist was rising up from the water, creating dancing clouds that the sun quickly burned away. My friends and I had been diving together for years, and this morning was perfect for another day in the clear water off Palm Beach.

By 8:00 A.M. we had untied the boat and

started down the intracoastal waterway toward an inlet that led to the open sea. The entire coast of Florida has a barrier island that protects the mainland from the ocean waves, and there are only a few places to go through it to reach the open ocean.

My favorite diving friend, a man called Amos, looks like Santa Claus. He has a long white beard and a shock of white hair to match.

Amos is sixty years old but still loves to dive every chance he gets. He is always happy and laughing and makes our diving days full of fun. Today he seemed especially good-humored as he steered our boat to the sea.

Diving off the coast of Florida is different from diving most other places because the water consists of a moving river within the Atlantic Ocean called the Gulf Stream. The Gulf Stream

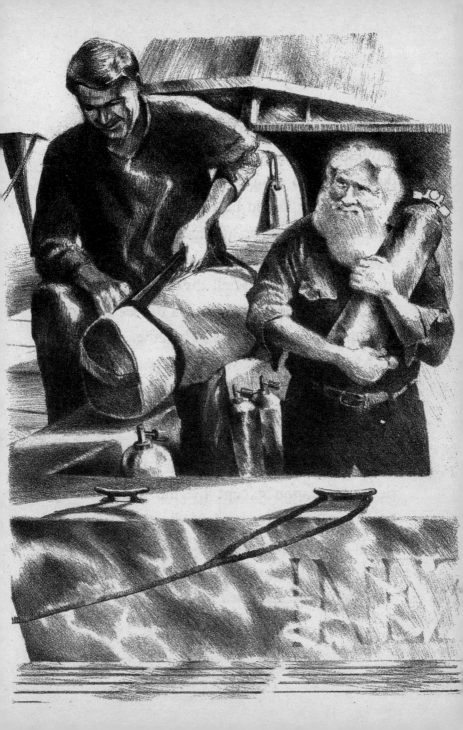

runs from south to north along the Florida coast, providing divers with a free ride as long as they don't try to go against the current.

Today we would be using scuba (self-contained underwater breathing apparatus) to dive along the offshore reefs between sixty and a hundred feet deep. Each diver wears a single tank of compressed air with a device called a regulator that allows him to breathe.

Most of the divers with us were there to hunt for big fish. These divers carry spear guns with which to shoot fish to take home for dinner.

I was there to dive purely for pleasure and for the beauty of the underwater sea, so I carried no weapon except for the usual diving knife every diver wears in a sheath strapped to his or her leg near the ankle, for use only in emergency situations.

That morning the sea was as smooth as glass

with no waves and no wind blowing at all.

With the mist rising up and the sun beating down to warm our bodies, it was a very special morning.

By the time we reached our diving area, we were all ready in our rubber wet suits, which would keep us warm in the sea's cool depths, and were outfitted with our scuba gear. Our flippers were on our feet, our masks on our heads ready to put over our eyes and noses when we got into the ocean.

As I looked down into the water, I could see the bottom approximately eighty feet under the boat. It was perfectly clear; the sky was a deep blue, and the air was cool and comfortable.

There had been other perfect days, but for some reason, that day was like no other.

Chapter Two

Down into the Blue Sea

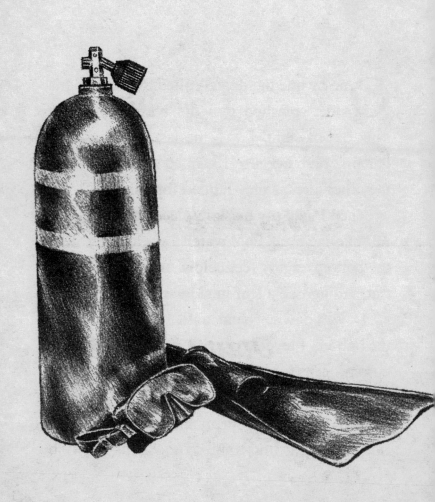

O ne by one the divers rolled over the boat's side, splashed into the water, and soon sank out of sight. I was the last overboard for the first dive because I wanted to stay clear of the other men as they hunted for fish.

Then I held my mask in place and let myself fall into the clear, cool water. I started to sink to the bottom, eighty feet below, and as I did, I lay flat, falling like a leaf in slow motion.

Down, down I went until I was just above the bottom. I leveled off and let the Gulf Stream current gently push me northward along the reef.

The beauty that surrounded me was like a fairyland that morning. Thousands of fish

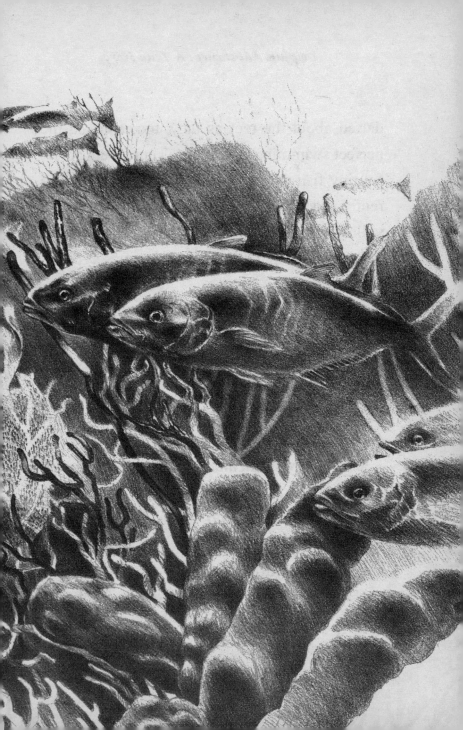

darted about the reef as they, too, enjoyed the perfect swimming conditions. There were colorful tiny fish darting in and out of the coral and reef rocks. There were large schools of jacks, yellow-tailed snappers, and grunts moving in unison as if marching to an army sergeant's command.

I saw a school of barracudas flashing by like a hundred sharp, shiny sea knives as they tried to run down their breakfast. Beneath my feet two stingrays scurried along the sea bottom, flapping their big wings like giant bats of the deep. It was nature on parade.

As I lazily swam along, I had a deep sense of peace. I was in the world of fish where there were no telephones, no traffic lights, and no noise from the busy land world up above. It was silent and beautiful.

Each minute I saw new wonders. Lobsters

peered from their hiding places, waving their long feelers like pairs of giant whiskers in the passing sea. Near one lobster nest, a huge green moray eel stuck its pointed nose out to greet me, opening and closing its mouth to breathe water through its gills.

I thought of all the stories I had heard about the moray eel's being dangerous because earlier divers thought its open mouth was like a dog snarling. They were wrong. The morays, like most other sea creatures, are friendly and harmless when treated with respect.

For thirty-five minutes I enjoyed the beauty of the dive, rising and falling as the current pushed me along. Suddenly two big nurse sharks, startled by my presence, shot from an overhang in the reef and disappeared out of sight. Their strength and beauty were a joy to behold as I watched them swim away.

It was a perfect day, a perfect dive, but now as I looked at my watch and my gauges, I knew I had to go back to the surface to join my diving friends and rest up before the second dive.

I climbed slowly, not wanting to leave the sea floor behind. Then my head broke water, and I could see the blue sky with seabirds whirling about in search of a fish dinner.

The boat spotted me, and I was soon on board, stowing my equipment and comparing notes with the other divers. They had each brought up several large fish, which flopped about on the boat's floor.

Chapter Three

A Strange Feeling

After an hour we were ready for a second dive. For some reason I had a strange feeling about it.

Although the others suited up and dived right in, I waited and asked Amos to take me farther north along the outer reef. I don't know why I wanted to go there, but I felt myself being pulled in that direction.

Amos laughed and said, "You can dive anywhere you want to. Just be sure you carry a float ball so I can find you."

The float ball is a large, bright orange plastic ball attached to a long rope a diver carries. The ball stays on the surface. That way the dive boat can keep track of where each diver is.

Geared up and ready to dive, I held the end of the rope in my hand, and when we got to the place I felt was right, I rolled over the side of the boat and into the water.

As I drifted down, I had the distinct feeling that something was happening over which I had no control. I tried to relax, but the feeling would not go away.

After swimming along the deep outer reef edge at eighty feet, I suddenly

heard a loud clicking noise in the water. It grew louder with each passing second.

I stopped and held on to a large rock as I tried to see what was making the noise. I looked in every direction.

The clicking became so loud, I could feel it against my eardrums. There was something familiar about the noise, but I could not place it.

Then I saw them!

Racing through the clear water, three dolphins were coming from the deep side of the reef, knifing through the water with graceful speed.

Chapter Four

The Dolphins

I had been diving for many years, but never before had wild dolphins come near me)in the water.

As I watched, the three swam closer to me.

There was a large male, a smaller female, and a baby dolphin. As the three circled me, I could see the baby was bleeding from a deep wound near its tail where a long string of clear plastic fishing line trailed for several feet behind.

The male and female dolphins were making a clicking noise as they swam nearer to me. Then they stopped and hovered.

The clicking noise also stopped.

The baby was between its mother and father. All three looked at me with their little eyes over upturned mouths, reminding me of a human grin.

I could see the baby had become tangled in a fishing line with a big hook that had snagged it between the dorsal fin on its back and the tail fluke. The shaft of the hook was sticking out of the bleeding wound, making a trail of green in the depth.

Because all colors are filtered out in the ocean depth, the baby's red blood looked green eighty feet below the surface. My first reaction was one of awe. My second thought was worry for the baby. I knew it would either get snagged and drown or be tracked down and eaten by a shark.

Dolphins are very intelligent and are abundantly happy in their wild domain. They are loving and loyal and have close family ties, taking care of their young and their older, less able peers.

They seldom approach people in the sea

and with good reason. Humans are dangerous and can cause them harm. But these dolphins were desperate.

The baby dolphin looked scared and in pain. Its little eyes rolled in their sockets as it watched me. It was afraid of me, but its parents had brought it near. I looked into the eyes of each of them as they hovered just three feet away, and thought about all the dolphins that had been needlessly killed by fishermen and their nets or caught on their hooks. All my life I have loved animals and have done my best to see they are respected and protected. Perhaps the dolphins had sensed that I was a friend. There were four other divers in the water, all armed with weapons. I was alone and unarmed.

Now we were face-to-face. This dolphin family had an injured baby. Could they have come to me for help?

I knew something most unusual was happening.

The baby dolphin would probably die without help, but what could I do? How could I do anything about the fishing hook and the plastic line?

I had only my big diving knife and no one to help me. If I didn't help, the baby was doomed. I decided I must try.

I reached out to touch the big male, who was nearest me, and all three suddenly shot away, swimming out of sight.

I felt a great surge of disappointment thinking I'd never see them again. Had I done something wrong?

Then, within seconds, they were back. They swam around me, clicking again, but more softly. They kept their eyes on me every moment. Now I was convinced the dolphins had chosen me to help them.

I tied the rope from the float ball to a nearby rock and let myself sink to the sea floor, where I sat on my knees.

I could sense the dolphins were trying to communicate with me. As I sat there on the sea bottom looking at the three creatures, I knew it was a rare moment. They were trusting me and I was trusting them. With their great speed and strength, they could easily injure me.

They needed help, but they could not speak. I wanted them to know I would help, but I could not communicate in their dolphin language. There must be a way, but how?

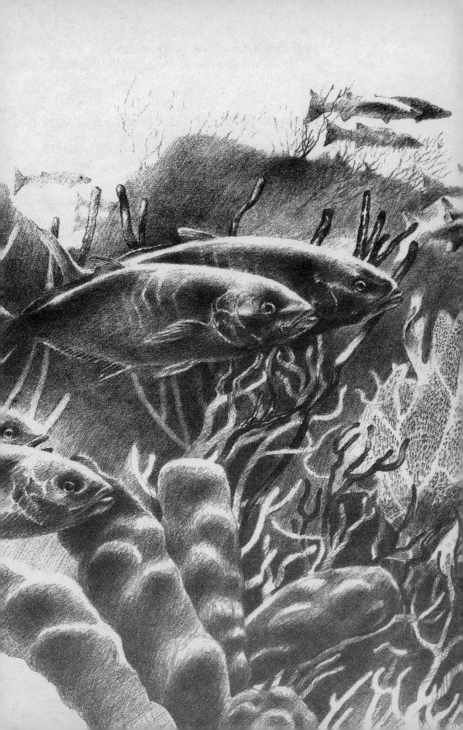

Chapter Five

I Try to Help

The clicking increased in frequency and then stopped. The three dolphins moved very slowly toward me. With their strong tail flukes barely moving up and down, they inched nearer and nearer until they were close enough for me to reach out and touch them.

The mother and father dolphin were slightly above the baby and were holding it between their flippers as they tried to place it on the sand right in front of me. At last they pushed the baby to the bottom.

The baby was frightened, and I could see it trembling. Its eyes never left mine. I slowly reached out to touch it, but when I did, it freed itself and swam rapidly away. The two parent dolphins immediately swam after it. In moments they were back, holding the baby tightly between them.

The father dolphin, hovering just inches from me, placed his nose under my arm and pushed up. My arm lifted, and I let it fall back in place. Again the big dolphin lifted it. I looked at his upturned mouth and bright eyes and couldn't help smiling. The impatient father dolphin wanted me to "get to work."

I took off my diving gloves and slowly reached out to touch the trembling baby. Its skin was smooth and silky as I ran my hand from just behind its breathing hole on the top of its head to the base of its dorsal fin in the middle of its back. I used my fingers to stroke its nose very gently, then ran them up and between its eyes.

The trembling stopped as the little dolphin

began to sense that I had no intention of harming it. After petting it for a couple of minutes, I slowly ran my hand to the wounded area near its tail. The clear fishing line was wrapped around the thin part of its body, embedded into the skin, causing blood to ooze out.

The shaft of the fishhook stuck out from a bloody hole in its back that had been ripped open when the baby broke the line, freeing itself from the fisherman above.

It was in great pain and frightened. Instinctively it understood that a shark could sniff along the blood trail and find it. That would be the end of the baby dolphin, and all four of us knew it.

I knew that getting the hook out and the line loose would be painful for the baby, but it had to be done.

All I had to work with was the big diving

knife I wore strapped to my right leg. It was about a foot long, and it was not very sharp.

I gently touched the hook shaft, and the baby made a high-pitched cry. It was going to be hard to help it.

Suddenly all three dolphins swam away, climbing toward the surface above. I had forgotten they had to breathe every few minutes.

Within a minute they were right back to me, this time with the baby coming along on its own. I knew I had to work fast so they could breathe when they needed to.

Chapter Six

Surgery on the
Sea Floor

I gently held the baby on the sea floor, then cut the trailing fishing line free until all that was left was the part embedded under the baby's tender skin. Getting it out with as little pain for the baby as possible was going to be the hard part.

Then, bit by bit, I started pulling the embedded line loose so I could cut it with my knife. As I pulled it up, more blood flowed out.

I looked around for sharks, not wanting to get in the way if the parent dolphins needed to protect their baby from an attack.

Seeing no sharks, I gently continued to pull some line free.

The baby cried out in pain, and the big dolphin clicked several times. It seemed as though the parent dolphins were working with me, encouraging their baby to cooperate.

Finally, all the line was cut free except for a short piece attached to the hook. This was going to be the hardest part. I touched the hook shaft, and the baby jumped and trembled. I carefully ran my finger into the deep wound, feeling its body heat within the flesh. The baby struggled to get away, but I placed my left hand on its back and pushed it down against the sand.

I felt so bad to be hurting it, but I knew if I didn't help, it would probably die.

Holding the baby dolphin with my left hand, I stuck one finger down the hook shaft until I felt the place where it turned up to form the barbed hook. It was stuck tight, hooked into the muscle tissue in the baby's tail.

I tried to wiggle it free, but it would not budge.

As the baby cried out, the mother dolphin

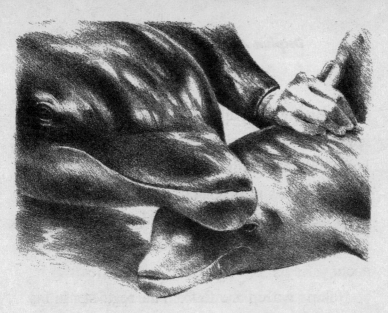

used her nose to stroke the baby, calming its struggle. She watched my hands closely and seemed like a nurse hovering over a doctor at the operating table.

The hook had to be cut free, and I dreaded using the big diving knife to do it, but there was no choice.

Placing the blade between my fingers the way you would hold a pencil to write, I very carefully put the point into the hole above the embedded hook.

The baby cried and struggled. I could not hold it with my hand, so I placed my left leg over its body and held it down gently. I stroked its whole body for a few moments, trying to calm it.

Impatient, the big dolphin again nudged me with his bottle nose. They would need to breathe soon.

Taking a deep breath from the regulator in my mouth, I slipped the knife into the wound and gently ran it down along the hook shaft. I used my left hand to feel into the wound as I pushed the knife in. Then I hit the muscle tissue that held the hook in place. It was now or never.

I cut the barb loose, and the hook was free. I withdrew the knife and took the hook out. Blood flowed from the baby's tail, and I pushed my palm down hard on the open wound to slow the bleeding.

Chapter Seven

The Dolphin's Thanks

The two big dolphins clicked excitedly about me. I felt a great surge of relief. I had done it. My heart was filled with joy. I was unbelievably happy.

Then the big dolphin suddenly darted away downcurrent. Something had caught his attention. A pair of bull sharks were coming straight for the baby, sniffing the blood trail as it flowed toward them in the fast Gulf Stream.

The father dolphin saw them and raced for them head-on. He was so fast that even the speeding sharks could not get out of his way.

Wham! The father dolphin hit the bigger shark right behind its gill slits, knocking it aside.

Wham! He hit it again. The shark swam away with a trail of blood pouring from its gills. It wanted no more fight with the protective father dolphin.

The other shark continued swimming straight toward the baby and me. The mother dolphin exploded into action. She tore through the water and met the shark with a fierce bump to its side.

A second later the father dolphin hit it from the other side. It swam away, also trailing blood.

The father dolphin followed, making repeated attacks, ensuring they would not return to harm the bleeding baby.

The sharks were no match for the enraged parent dolphins who had saved their baby and probably me, too.

I lifted my hand from the baby, and the bleeding had almost stopped. The mother dolphin had returned. She looked at the hole in its body and then at the hook lying on the sand nearby. She clicked loudly, and I heard more clicking from farther away. It was the father dolphin coming back.

He had chased the sharks far away. He was there in an instant, swimming rapidly back to his family.

I let the baby up, and it joined the parent dol-

phins. They all swam around me, making clicking sounds.

The father dolphin swam right up to me and looked into my eyes behind the diving mask. He nodded his head up and down in a rapid motion and then gently pushed me with his nose.

I reached out to touch his head, and he let me do so. For that brief moment, whether it was my imagination or it was really happening, I had the strong impression that he was thanking me, one father to another.

Then he made the clicking sound again, and the three swam rapidly toward the surface, leaving me alone on the bottom. I knew it was time for them to breathe again.

I looked at my air gauge and saw I had enough air to swim awhile longer. The experience that I will never forget had all happened in about ten minutes.

THE DOLPHIN'S THANKS

I kept looking for the dolphins to return that day, but they didn't.

As I climbed into the boat after I surfaced, I felt a happiness that I have never known before. The dolphins had left me with a sense of peace and a strong feeling of love.

Chapter Eight

The Dolphins Return

All the way back from the day's dive, I could not stop feeling the dolphins were still communicating with me from someplace out there in the sea.

For the next couple of weeks I kept thinking about the baby dolphin, wondering if the sharks had gotten it or if it had survived. I couldn't get the dolphins out of my mind.

Then Amos called to see if I wanted to dive the next morning, and I said yes.

It was a different kind of morning from that last time. The sky was overcast, and the sea was much rougher with a cool northeastern wind blowing whitecaps toward shore. Only Amos and one other diver were along as we sped down

the coast to our selected diving area.

I was working on my diving equipment when Amos shouted, "Hey, look over there. Dolphins!"

I looked up, and sure enough, several dolphins were racing with our boat, jumping from the water right by our bow wake. Suddenly I had that same feeling I had experienced on the day I helped the dolphin family.

Then I saw a small dolphin. It was in the midst of six other dolphins with a scar clearly visible on its back. It was the baby I had helped. I cheered and laughed until the tears rolled down my cheeks. The baby dolphin had survived.

It swam close to the boat, easily keeping pace with our speed, jumping high out of the water. It seemed its upturned mouth had an even bigger grin on it than before.

For a few minutes the dolphins stayed with us. Then they swam away, jumping and enjoying just being alive in the sea.

As I watched them go, I knew I had experienced something very special.

It's been some time now since my dolphin adventure, but I often think about that dolphin family. I shall never forget the feeling of happiness I felt in their presence.

I look forward to swimming with the dolphins again. It could happen anytime now.

Wayne Grover was born in Minneapolis, Minnesota. He is a veteran of the United States Air Force and has travelled the world during and after his twenty-five-year military career. He is an active conservationist and an avid parachutist, a scuba diver, white water rafter, hiker, and naturalist. He has worked on shark research in the Pacific, and at present his chief interests are marine research and historical wrecks.

Now a freelance journalist, his articles on conservation and ecological balance have appeared in newspapers and magazines throughout the world. This is his first book for children.

He lives with his wife, Barbara, in Florida.

Jim Fowler began drawing his horse when he was a youngster growing up in Tulsa, Oklahoma. His interest in observing animals has taken him to wild places in much of North America and in 1973 brought him to Alaska, where he has lived ever since. He enjoys hiking, kayaking, and living near the ocean.

He has illustrated several pieces for *Highlights for Children* and is the illustrator of *The Secret Moose* by Jean Rogers.

He lives in Juneau with his wife, Susi Gregg Fowler, and their daughters, Angela and Micaela.